Joe Van der Katt and the Great Picket Fence

Joe Van der Katt and the Great Picket Fence

by Peter J. Welling

PELICAN PUBLISHING COMPANY
Gretna 2005

To Gerard M. "Dutch" Welling and Margaret M. Springer Welling,
who were proud members of blue-collar, middle-class America

And to Darlene, baker of my banket staven

Dank u *to Joseph P. Welling, Theo Kooij, Ph.D., and his daughter Nina for the Dutch translations*

Library of Congress Cataloging-in-Publication Data

Welling, Peter J.
  Joe Van Der Katt and the great picket fence / by Peter J. Welling.
      p. cm.
  Summary: In the town of Litterbox in New York's Catskill Mountains, the fat cats have all of the money and power until the poor cats get organized and demand fair pay and better working conditions.
  ISBN 9781589802810 (alk. paper)
  [1. Labor unions—Fiction. 2. Cats—Fiction. 3. Catskill Mountains Region (N.Y.)—Fiction. 4. New York (State)—History—Fiction. 5. Humorous stories.] I. Title.

  PZ7.W4573Jo 2005
  [Fic]—dc22

                                  2004022086

Printed in Singapore
Published by Pelican Publishing Company, Inc.
1000 Burmaster Street, Gretna, Louisiana 70053

Joe Van der Katt and the Great Picket Fence

The legend of Joe Van der Katt began long ago in the town of Litterbox, a Dutch settlement in the Catskill Mountains of New York. In the poor section of Litterbox lived Joe Van der Katt and his wife, Mary Lu.

The Van der Katts lived in a crate under a creaky catwalk. Their friends, Wobbly and Gompers, lived catty-corner from them in a cardboard box. Across town lived the rich kitties. They were known as the Fat Cats.

The top cat in Litterbox was J. Paul Kitty. He owned wildcat oil wells, the Cattanooga choo-choo, a Catawba-grape vineyard, and the Cat's Cradle Company. He was so rich that he hired poor cats to meow for him.

Joe, Wobbly, and Gompers worked at the Cat's Cradle Company. They made gorgeous girls' beds from pussy-willow wood. They made beautiful boys' beds from catalpa trees. The cats worked hard but were paid just pennies a day.

Since Fat Cats owned most of the stores in town, the poor cats had no choice on where to shop. They bought meat and milk from Andrew Catnegie's Cattle Company, canned goods from Cathy's Cannery, and coal from Baron Calico.

One night as they dined on Cheesy Mouseburger Helper with Hairballs, Mary Lu said, "Joe, we need more money. All of the working cats need more money. *You* need to ask Mr. Kitty to give everyone a raise."

"Oh, no," Joe howled. "Bad idea. Do you remember Jack Catillac? He once asked for a raise. What a catastrophe that was. Mr. Kitty's bullyboys packed Jack into a barrel and sent it over Kaaterskill Falls."

"Don't worry, you old fraidy-cat," Mary Lu said. "When cats fall they always land on their feet. You should worry about important things. We have nothing to burn for heat this coming winter except a stack of Cat's Cradle catalogs."

J. Paul Kitty sat behind his large desk in his large office. Joe's tail twitched nervously. "Well?" Mr. Kitty roared. "What's the matter—cat got your tongue?"

"I—I need a raise," Joe finally squeaked.

"Why?" Mr. Kitty howled. "So you can squander it on catnip?"

"Oh, no," Joe said. "All of the factory cats need more money. My wife said so. We can't afford wood for heat, food to eat, or shoes for our feet."

"Cat's paw!" Mr. Kitty yelled. "No raises. However, if you want to earn some extra money, I can tell you how."

"They say curiosity killed the cat," Joe gulped. "But go ahead, tell me."

"I guess we could," Joe replied. He was then catapulted through the window by the bad bullyboys and landed on his tail. "Me-owww," he howled. "I thought cats always landed on their feet."

"That's an old wives' tale," Mr. Kitty said.

WEZEL.

Though it was raining cats and dogs, hundreds of cats poured onto the field to harvest the grapes. When the last Catawba was picked, Joe declared, "I'll go get our money."

"Good," Gompers said. "We're wet, hungry, and need catnaps."

"How many baskets of grapes were picked?" J. Paul Kitty asked.

"Two hundred and nine," Joe said.

"And how many of those baskets did *you* pick by yourself?" Mr. Kitty asked.

"Me? I picked ten of them," Joe said.

"Then here is fifty cents," Mr. Kitty told him.

"What about the other cats?" Joe asked.

"Oh," Mr. Kitty said, "I promised to pay *you*, not them." He grinned and rode away.

"All cats to Debs' Diner!" Joe shouted. "Soup's on me."

"That old sourpuss will want us to make girl cots and boy cots on Monday, just like nothing happened," Joe said. "What should we do?"

"Nothing strikes me," Wobbly sighed, slurping his soup.

"I'm striking out as well," added Gompers.

Sadly, the cats reported for work on Monday. "Joe," Mr. Kitty said, "some of these workers seem upset. Now, I'm no scaredy-cat, but maybe we should build a fence around my factory, just in case."

"You have to pay each fence-building cat ten cents a day," Joe declared.

"Oh, sure," Mr. Kitty said. Soon a ten-foot-tall picket fence surrounded the factory.

"Our pay, please," Joe said.

"We agreed on a penny a day, right?" Mr. Kitty asked.

"Ten cents a day," Joe insisted. Mr. Kitty hissed. The bullyboys charged, but to their surprise, there was no gate.

"Get a ladder," Mr. Kitty sputtered. Soon the bullyboys were over the fence. They chased the cats into Chatty's Cattery.

"Hello, hamburger," a voice from the dark said. Someone lit a candle. The bullyboys' eyes popped wide open. There were lions and tigers and barely enough room for Joe to squeeze through.

"Hi, bullyboys," Joe called. "Meet the cat union."

The bullyboys never returned to the factory, but the cats did. They started walking along the top of the fence, chanting as they went, "Two, four, six, eight. Give us our money; we'll give you the gate." Mr. Kitty just laughed.

Days passed. Soon there was a picket fence full of cats.
"What about the girl beds?" Mr. Kitty whined. "What about the boy cots?"

"Fzzt," they hissed. "Two, four, six, eight . . ."

"Yeah, yeah," Mr. Kitty said. "I know."

POMPOEN...?

No beds were made. Mr. Kitty was losing a lot of money. "I give up!" he cried. "I'll pay for the fence and the grape picking and even give a hair-raising raise."

The cats lay down on the fence. "Purr-fect," they purred.

The cats celebrated at Debs' Diner. "I wonder if years from now cats will remember this day?" Joe asked.

The answer is yes. In fact, cats celebrate Lay-Purr Day all year long.

Glossary

page 4: banket staven (ban-KEHT STAV-uhn)—pastries in the shape of alphabet letters

page 5: rijtuig (RAY-towg)—carriage

page 6: kat (kat)—cat

page 7: melk (mehlk)—milk

page 8: muis (mowss)—mouse

page 9: waarschuwing (VAHR-skow-ing)—warning

page 10: molen (MO-luhn)—windmill

page 11: stieren (steern)—bulls; meer (mayr)—lake

page 12: brood (brote)—bread; Gouda (GOW-duh)—a Dutch cheese

page 13: kaas (kahss)—cheese

page 14: koe (koo)—cow; appel (AP-puhl)—apple

page 15: haas (hahss)—hare

page 16: haan (hahn)—rooster

page 17: bever (BAY-vuhr)—beaver

page 18: wezel (VAY-zuhl)—weasel

page 19: vleermuis (VLAYR-mowss)—bat

page 20: hete chocolade (HAY-tuh sho-ko-LAH-duh)—hot chocolate

page 21: verwelkomen (vuhr-VEHL-ko-muhn)—welcome

page 22: soep (soop)—soup

page 23: slang (slang)—snake

page 24: natte verf (NAT-tuh vehrf)—wet paint